A VERY SPECIAL CRITTER

BY GINA AND MERCER MAYER

For Caroline Hall

A GOLDEN BOOK • NEW YORK
Western Publishing Company, Inc., Racine, Wisconsin 53404

Library of Congress Catalog Card Number: 92-72988. ISBN: 0-307-12763-X / ISBN: 0-307-62763-2 (lib. bdg.)
MCMXCIII

One day my teacher said, "A new critter
is coming to our class tomorrow."

I was glad. I hoped the new critter
would be someone really cool.

Then my teacher said, "Our new student is a very special critter. He can't walk, so he uses a wheelchair. I want you all to try very hard to make him feel at home."

I was a little scared because I had never known anyone in a wheelchair before.

I told my dad about it. He said, "Just because he's in a wheelchair doesn't mean he's any different than the rest of you. He probably just needs some special help once in a while."

I thought that made sense.

The next day they brought the new student
to our class. He looked scared.

But his wheelchair was really cool. It had stickers of dinosaurs and funny monsters all over it.

My teacher said, "This is our new student. Alex, we are very happy to have you in our class."

Then we all introduced ourselves.

I was curious about Alex. So was everyone else. At recess we all talked to Alex. Some critters asked him questions about his wheelchair.

He didn't seem to mind.

At first everyone in the class thought
Alex needed a lot of help.

We were wrong.

He can go almost anywhere he wants in his wheelchair. Once in a while he needs a little push to get over a bump.

His wheelchair can't go up stairs, so
he rolls it up the special ramp at school.

His wheelchair has pouches to carry
his books and things he needs for school.
Sometimes he even carries *my* books for me.

Sometimes Alex needs help reaching things way up high. Sometimes I do; too.

He plays games in the playground with the rest of us. When we play dodgeball, he always gets the most people out.

And he's great at volleyball.

He does have
a little trouble with
hide-and-seek, though.

Alex rides a special bus. It has a lift that takes his wheelchair up and down.

We take turns helping him to the bus.

Alex likes the same things my other friends like. He plays with race cars and dinosaurs and he loves Super Critter.

For our Halloween party at school,
Alex dressed up like a car. He had
the best costume in the whole school.

He's a good artist, too.
He won an art contest at
school and our class got
an ice cream party.

Once in a while
something will come up
that Alex needs help with.

But it's no big deal.
Sometimes I need him
to help me, too.

My dad was right about Alex.
Even though he's a special critter,
he's just one of the gang.